JEREMY'S DREIDEL

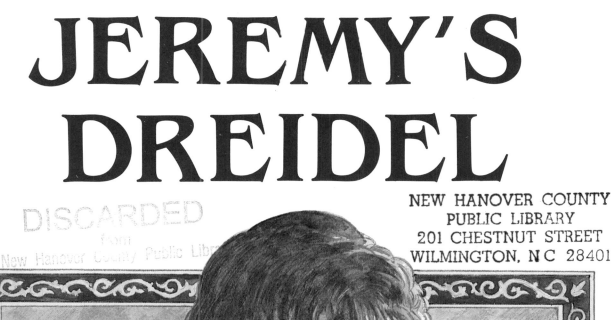

Ellie Gellman
illustrated by Judith Friedman

KAR-BEN COPIES, INC.   ROCKVILLE, MD

For Abba
who was a real good listener
—EG

Library of Congress Cataloging-in-Publication Data

Gellman, Ellie
    Jeremy's dreidel/Ellie Gellman; illustrated by Judith Friedman.
      p.   cm.
    Summary: Jeremy signs up for a Hanukkah workshop to make unusual dreidels and creates a clay
dreidel with braille dots for his dad, who is blind.
    ISBN 0-929371-33-X (HC):   —ISBN 0-929371-34-8 (pbk.):
    [1. Dreidel (Game)—Fiction. 2. Handicraft—Fiction. 3. Hanukkah—Fiction. 4.Jews—Fiction.
5. Blind—Fiction. 6. Physically handicapped—Fiction. 7. Fathers and sons—Fiction.]
I. Friedman, Judith, 1945- ill. II. Title.
P27.G2835Je 1992
[Fic]—dc20   92-11427
                                                                            CIP
                                                                            AC

JEREMY'S DREIDEL

"SIGN UP FOR HANUKKAH CRAFT CLASSES!" Jeremy read the big yellow poster in the Jewish Center display case. One of the classes sounded interesting. "A dreidel doesn't have to be made of wood or plastic," the sign said. "What would you use? Bring your ideas to Different Dreidels, Monday at 4 PM." Jeremy thought for a minute, then wrote his name on the sign up sheet.

When he arrived on Monday, Jeremy recognized a few others in the art room. Abby, who used to be in his carpool, was carrying a box filled with paper towel tubes and old magazines. David, from Jeremy's swimming class, was looking through a book.

''Come look at this science experiment,'' he called to Jeremy. ''It's a black and white top that turns colors when you spin it. Do you think I can make a dreidel like that?''

''Sure you can,'' said a friendly voice. ''I'm Miriam, your art teacher.''

Everyone found seats around the table. ''We're here to make original and interesting dreidels,'' Miriam said. ''But first do we all know what a dreidel is?''

Adam spoke first. ''It's a top, and we spin it to play a Hanukkah game.''

''It has four Hebrew letters on it,'' Jeremy added. ''*Nun, Gimel, Hey,* and *Shin.* They stand for *Nes Gadol Hayah Sham,* A Great Miracle Happened There.''

"That's right," Miriam smiled. "Hanukkah celebrates the victory of the small Maccabee army over the huge army of Antiochus. That was a miracle."

"There was another miracle," said Jacob. "When the Maccabees lit the Temple menorah, the tiny jar of oil lasted for eight whole days. That's why we light candles for eight days."

"My name is Orit and I was born in Israel," said a girl with short, curly hair. "We call a dreidel a sevivon. The letters on an Israeli sevivon say A Great Miracle Happened *Here*. I'm going to put those letters on my dreidel."

"What ideas do the rest of you have?" Miriam asked the group.

Abby emptied her bag on the table. "These are things that people usually throw away. I want to recycle them and make an environmentally-friendly dreidel," she explained.

David asked Miriam to help him with the dreidel that changes colors. Jacob had brought a music box from an old toy to make a singing dreidel. Matthew wanted to use a rubber ball so his dreidel would bounce.

"What do you need for your dreidel?" Miriam asked Jeremy.

"Just clay," he said simply.

"Do you want to look through my science book for a more interesting idea?" David asked.

"No thanks," Jeremy replied, as he returned from the supply closet with a lump of gray clay. "I have a great idea already. My dreidel is a surprise for someone."

Jeremy began rolling, pounding, and softening the clay, concentrating hard.

David tried to keep his mind on sanding his wood, but he couldn't stop looking over at Jeremy. He wondered what kind of surprise someone could make from a lump of clay.

Soon Adam became curious, too. He peeked over Jeremy's shoulder. "Look at this!" he called out. A group gathered to watch, as Jeremy carefully molded tiny dots onto the sides of his dreidel.

"Wow!" exclaimed Jacob. "What's that? A secret code?"

Jeremy looked up. He expected his friends would be curious. He was used to explaining. He just hoped they would understand.

"The dots are called Braille," he answered. "It's a way of reading for blind people. This group of dots is a *Nun.* The others will be *Gimel, Hey,* and *Shin.*"

"I know about Braille," said Sally. "Blind people can't see the letters on a piece of paper, or the numbers on a watch, but they can feel dots with their fingers. The dots stand for letters and words."

"Who do you know who is blind?" Adam asked Jeremy. "You said you were making a surprise for someone."

"It's for my dad," Jeremy answered quietly.

Jeremy's friends all began to talk at once.

"I didn't know your dad was blind," said David.

"How can he help you with your homework?" wondered Orit.

"But you don't have a dog," said Abby.

"Not all blind people have dogs," Jeremy answered. "My dad uses a cane to be sure he doesn't bump into anything. He reads Braille books and magazines, and he even uses a Braille prayer book in the synagogue. When he helps me with my math homework, he does long division in his head!"

"But what does he do all day?" Matthew wondered.

"He goes to work, just like your mom and dad," said Jeremy. "And in his free time he sings in the choir here at the JCC."

"I still don't understand how he can be blind," insisted David. "When I come over to play, he always says hi and knows my name. Besides he doesn't look blind."

"Blind isn't how you look, it's how you see," Jeremy said, impatiently. "And Dad knows all my friends' voices. He's a real good listener."

Jeremy looked around. Everyone seemed to be staring at him. And they had so many questions.

"I think I don't want to talk about it anymore," he said.

There was an awkward silence. The group was relieved when Miriam announced that it was time to stop. They'd have to finish on Wednesday.

Miriam sat down with Jeremy as the group cleaned up.

"Don't be sorry that you told the kids about your dad," she said.

"I didn't want to cause a problem," Jeremy said.

"I don't think you caused a problem at all," she reassured him. "It's hard for people to imagine being different, but it's very important to learn... much more important than how to make dreidels."

On Wednesday, while the class was busy painting and decorating their dreidels, Miriam made an announcement.

''The art department has decided to put some of your original dreidels in the lobby showcase for the Hanukkah Celebration on Sunday. I wish I could display them all, but they've asked for only three. Why don't we all vote for the ones we like best.''

A few minutes later, Miriam announced the group's choices: Abby's Environmentally-Friendly Dreidel, Jacob's Musical Dreidel, and Jeremy's Braille Dreidel.

Abby and Jacob beamed as the others congratulated them, but Jeremy slid down in his seat.

"What's wrong, Jeremy?" asked Miriam, surprised at his reaction.

"You don't understand," he said in a sad voice.

"Won't your dad be proud of you when he finds out your dreidel was chosen as the best?" asked Sally.

Jeremy tried to answer calmly. "He can't be proud of my dreidel in a display case," he explained. "He can't see it there, and he can't play with a dreidel that is locked behind glass."

The room was quiet for a long moment. Then a small voice spoke up. "Maybe Jeremy is right," said Abby. "Why do we need to put our dreidels in a showcase? Dreidels are to play with, not to look at."

"Instead of a display, why not put up posters inviting people to join us in a dreidel game," Jacob suggested.

"That's a great idea." Jeremy smiled. It felt great to know that his friends did understand after all.

The families who filled the JCC that Sunday afternoon enjoyed latkes and jelly doughnuts made by the cooking class. There was a play about Judah Maccabee, and Hanukkah songs led by the choir. Everyone noticed the dreidel-shaped posters on display. In huge black letters and in tiny raised dots they said:

TO FIND OUT HOW TO
MAKE UNUSUAL DREIDELS
JOIN US AT THE TABLE
NEAR THE WINDOW

The dreidel table was crowded as people picked up instruction sheets and joined in the games. Babies pulled the string on Jacob's dreidel to hear the music. Children sat in a circle to spin Abby's recycled dreidel. Even the grownups took turns with Jeremy's Braille dreidel and laughed as they tried

to read the letters. Jeremy sat with his father and his friends, smiling proudly. This is what I like best about Hanukkah, he thought. It's a time for everyone to celebrate together.

ABBY'S ENVIRONMENTALLY-FRIENDLY DREIDEL

Small Size

You will need:

Empty egg carton
Dried-out thin marker
Pictures from newspapers, magazines, or junk mail
Scissors, glue, dark marker

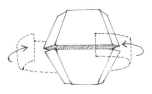

Cut two cups from the egg carton and tape them together at the open sides to make a ''ball''. Glue decorative pictures over the cups, making sure to cover the places where the two cups meet. Let the decorations dry. With a dark marker, write the Hebrew letters Nun, Gimmel, Hey, and Shin over the pictures, one on each side.

Poke the thin marker through the top and bottom of the ball. If the hole is too loose, reinforce it with tape. Let the point stick out a little on the bottom. When you play, the letter you have spun is the one that lands on top.

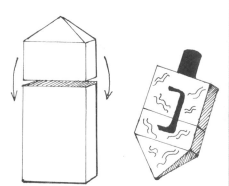

Large Size

You will need:

Empty milk carton, washed and dried
Pictures from newspapers, magazines, or junk mail
Dried-out fat marker
Scissors, glue, strong tape, marker

Cut the milk carton in half about 3'' from the spout. Bend the open spouts backwards, so that each side is flat against the carton. Tape them down. Open up the other side of the spout and bend those pieces backwards over the first. Tape them down as well. This should leave a point in the middle. Slide the spout half of the carton over the bottom half. Glue a collage of pictures on top of the cover. Let them dry and then write the Hebrew letters on the sides of the dreidel. Make a hole in the flat end of the milk carton. Poke the marker through for a handle (it will not reach the other end). Spin the dreidel and see which letter lands on top.

DAVID'S SCIENCE PROJECT DREIDEL

This dreidel uses an optical illusion called Benham's Wheel.

You will need:

Very short pencil with dull point
White cardboard circle or thin circle of wood, sanded smooth
Black marker and light-colored marker
4 small pieces of light-colored paper

With the black marker, copy this pattern of Benham's Wheel onto your circle. Make a hole in the center of the circle, and poke the pencil through. Only a little point needs to stick out. With the light marker, write the Hebrew letters on the pieces of colored paper, and glue onto the circle. When you spin the top, the black and white pattern will show colored stripes. The letter you have spun is the letter on the top.

MATTHEW'S DREIDEL BALL

You will need:

Old ball (small rubber, tennis or nerf ball)
Pen or pencil
Cardboard
Markers, scissors, glue

Cut a strip of cardboard about an inch wide, long enough to go around the ball with half an inch overlap. Mark off the half inch, and then fold the strip in half and in half again to make four even sides. Draw a dreidel letter on each side of the cardboard. Wrap the strip around the ball and tape the flap down.

Stick the pen into the top of the ball, letting most of it stick out on top. Spin the dreidel. It will roll and wobble and will eventually land with one of the letters on top.

HOW TO PLAY THE DREIDEL GAME

You will need a dreidel (any kind), and enough nuts, candies, chips, bottle caps, or pennies to give 10 to each player.

To start, each player puts one playing piece in the middle. The first player spins the dreidel. When it stops, look at the letter on top.

NUN ‎נ means *nothing*. You take nothing and lose nothing.

GIMMEL ‎ג means *get them all*. You take everything in the pile.

HEY ‎ה means *half*. You take half the pile. (If there is an uneven number, take half plus one.)

SHIN ‎שׁ means *share*. You must put another piece in the pile.

Any time all the pieces are gone, everyone must add one to the pile.

ABOUT BRAILLE

Braille letters are usually made by pushing out raised dots on heavy paper with a special Braille slate or typewriter. The number and position of dots changes for each letter. Each language has its own Braille alphabet. There are Braille books and magazines, and often Braille signs, elevator buttons, and captions on museum exhibits.

Jeremy used the Hebrew Braille alphabet on his dreidel. Here are the letters he used:

NUN ⠻ GIMEL ⠛ HEY ⠓ SHIN ⠱

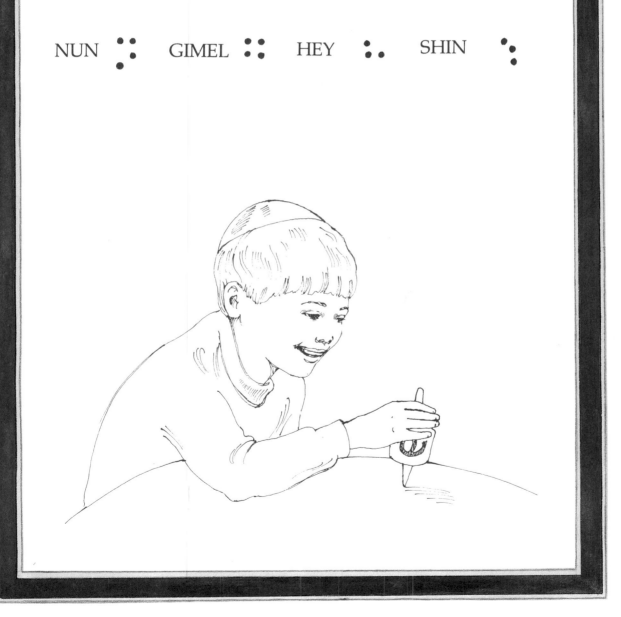

About the Author

Ellie Gellman grew up in Minneapolis. She and her husband Reuven, a research scientist, now live in Toronto with their four children, Shai, David, Avigail, and Michal. Ellie is Vice Principal for Hebrew Studies at United Synagogue Day Schools. She is the author of *Justin's Hebrew Name*, *Tamar's Sukkah*, and three toddler board books, all published by Kar-Ben.

About the Illustrator

Judith Friedman lives in Illinois with her husband David and their three cats, Amanda, Adele, and Celia. She studied art in her native France, and when she arrived in this country at the age of 17, continued her studies at the Art Institute of Chicago, where she later taught. In addition to illustrating children's books, Judith accepts commissions to do children's portraits.